The World's Biggest Fart
Somos8 Series

www.nubeocho.com – info@nubeocho.com

Original title: *El pedo más grande del mundo*
English translation: Kim Griffin
Text editing: Ben Dawlatly and Rebecca Packard
Special thanks to Fady Atallah

Distributed in the United States by
Consortium Book Sales & Distribution

First edition: 2017
ISBN: 978-84-945971-4-5

Printed in China by Asia Pacific Offset,
respecting international labor standards.

THE WORLD'S BIGGEST FART

Rafael Ordóñez Laure du Faÿ

The elephant sat on the riverbank. His feet sank into the mud, and he felt cool and refreshed. He closed his eyes with pleasure and drank some water slowly with his trunk.

“Ahhh! It’s great here! It’s so quiet and peaceful!”

BLURUP

All of a sudden the elephant heard a funny noise. He looked at the river and saw a great big bubble burst through the surface and explode into a smelly fart.

The huge fart had come from a huge hippo that suddenly poked his head above the water.

PRAGH

The elephant thought the hippo was a bit gross, even though the underwater fart was pretty funny.

Actually, the elephant's gigantic belly had been hurting a little. So, he looked at the hippo and let out a giant fart of his own that sounded like a clap of thunder.

The two large animals laughed for a long while without saying a single word, until a giraffe appeared. Without looking at them, she lowered her head to drink from the river.

As her head went down, her butt went up. And of course, she let out a fart. It was not particularly loud, but it was very, very long.

Just then a playful monkey, hanging upside down, called out between hoots of laughter,

“What an assortment of farts! You’re like the wind section of an orchestra.”

The giraffe blushed.

"I have a great idea," the monkey continued. "We could hold a farting contest."

The three animals just stood and stared at him. But then they heard the gruff voice of the crocodile:

"Very well. I'll be the judge."

The monkey disappeared into the trees yelling, "Farting contest tomorrow! At the river at noon. There's going to be a competition! A farting competition!"

Within minutes, all the jungle animals knew about the contest.

The next day, some animals were already hanging around the river before noon.

Pretty soon, the monkey began to shout,
"It's midday! It's midday! It's time to start...
it's time to fart!"

The crocodile glided to the bank and announced,

"Let the contest begin!"

The rhinoceros took his position in the center of all the other animals and, without a word, let out a loud fart. It wasn't an explosion, but you could tell it was a big, big, big fart (as big as the rhino himself).

All the animals cheered wildly, and the rhino was very proud.

In the river, the hippo squinted his eyes, wriggled his ears and fired an underwater bomb; a gigantic bubble burst behind him.

BLUP

The hippo grinned with delight
at the enthusiastic applause.

Then the zebra took center stage and said, “I hope you all can see that I’m smaller than the other contestants. Please don’t compare my effort to the rhino’s. I’m sure you’ll appreciate how refined my work is.”

And with a squeeze, she issued a series of small but perfectly formed farts, like firecrackers at a fireworks display.

CLAP
CLAP
CLAP
CLAP
PRT
PRT
PRT
PRT
PRT
PRT
CLAP
CLAP

After great applause for the zebra, it was the gazelle's turn. She was a little nervous. When she saw the leopard watching, smiling and licking his whiskers, the poor gazelle couldn't bear it anymore and popped out a tiny little nugget of poop.

"Disqualified," said the crocodile. "This is a farting contest."

PLOP

Silence descended as the gorilla started thumping his chest. With all the animals eagerly watching, he turned slowly and let out a small, barely audible fart.

No one applauded.

A small hedgehog said, “He thinks he’s such a scary gorilla but farts more like a little chinchilla.”

Everyone burst out laughing. The gorilla was mortified and left in a hurry.

At that moment the lion turned up, pushing the lioness forward.

“No way!” she protested. “You might be the king of the jungle, but you can’t ask me to do this. It’s enough that I hunt, feed and look after the little ones. So if you want to win this dumb competition, go ahead and fart your own fart.”

The elephant used this opportunity to grab the limelight. He pulled his belly in and let out a thunderous, resounding, monstrous bottom burp—a real gem of a fart that caused a tremendous uproar.

When the applause died down, the crocodile closed his eyes. Then he opened them and said, “After intense and deep reflection, the jury has decided that—”

OOMP

All the animals were astonished. They turned toward where the incredible sound had come from.

The rhino looked in the bushes and found the source of the most enormous fart that anyone had ever heard.

There in the bushes was a little mouse, rubbing his belly.
“Was it you who just farted?” asked the crocodile.
“You? Was it you?” the lion, gazelle, rhino, giraffe and monkey all repeated in disbelief.
“No way!” exclaimed all of the animals.

The poor little mouse was very embarrassed and began to shake.
What did it matter to all of them if he had farted or not?

But as they all kept on asking and insisting, demanding a reply, he couldn't take it anymore and yelled as loud as he could in his little rodent voice:

“Yes, it was me, okay?!
It was me who farted.
Sometimes it’s the only way
to fix a really sore tummy!”

The hippopotamus exclaimed:

“Such a tiny thing and he farts like a king!”

And all the animals cheered and applauded the little mouse king.